Grace C. Bibb

The Western

May 1876

Grace C. Bibb

The Western
May 1876

ISBN/EAN: 9783337049652

Printed in Europe, USA, Canada, Australia, Japan

Cover: Foto ©Andreas Hilbeck / pixelio.de

More available books at **www.hansebooks.com**

The Western.

MAY, 1876.

THE ENGLISH NOVEL—ITS ART VALUE.

IF all art attempts to seize spirit, it attempts no less to represent that which it has seized ; in the adequacy of the representation lies the measure of its value. The English Novel
if a work of art must be tried by the canons of art; if thus tried
it shall seem to possess real worth as an expression of
spirit, and if its final cause shall seem to be man's recognition
of himself, we shall have established a criterion of excellence ;
that will be the best novel which shall most perfectly interpret to man the problem of his spiritual life.

The germ of the novel is to be sought in the traditions of
illiterate peoples and in the mythologic ages. In those earlier
times semi-historic legends chanted in monotonous recitative
roused the passions of warriors or soothed the fatigues of the
chase; afterward it is probable that a certain decay of intellectual vigor not inconsistent with a somewhat more cultured
age led to the substitution of the prose style for the lyric form.
With greater diversity in the interests of the people and with
increasing complexity in the conditions of life the change became more general ; when other things than war claimed the
attention of nations, other themes than war found a place
even if subordinate in the chronicles of the time. Thus was

introduced the element of variety. Later a natural desire, on the part of its narrator to make his story as effective as might be led to the effort more or less conscious to bring out into stronger light the crises of the tale, to withdraw more and more into shade its subordinate incidents. Still later, in the rivalry of authors, which no doubt existed, skilful arrangement was of course supplemented by fictitious adornment, while such circumstances as impeded the progress of the action were lightly touched upon or wholly ignored. In these stories we must expect to find little discrimination of character; the thought of the time was busy with the material world, it had enough to do to support life, to gain food and shelter and comparative security; it could spend no time in introspection. Its heroes are, therefore, the men who stand for most when placed over against hunger and cold and the attacks of brute force; they are impersonations of courage, endurance, physical power; they illustrate the attitude of early peoples toward the existing order.

In time the romance proper follows tradition and precedes the novel. Its place of origin is probably Persia, whence through the Milesians it spread into Greece, having earlier found entrance into Italy. Yet it was adopted by the Greeks only when their truer literature had perished and when their liberties, no longer thought worthy of effectual defense, were about to be crushed by the Macedonian conqueror. Rome, too, amused herself with the stories of the East only when the causes of her ultimate downfall had begun to work out their legitimate results. The romance grew into power with the height and decline of the Empire. Among its representative authors are the Greeks, Antonius Diogenes, Heliodorus, Tatius and Longus, with some others. Heliodorus in Theogenes and Chariclea has furnished incident for the Jerusalem Delivered of Tasso. Some writers, too, we are told

by Dunlop, in his history of Fiction, trace a resemblance between the great work of Heliodorus and the modern novel
as represented by Richardson. Perhaps there is no other
point of similarity than that in both stories it is the heroine
who is the chief personage. Indeed it is stated as a curious
fact of all Classical Romances that in them woman is assigned
an ideal elevation and prominence glaringly in contrast with her
real position in the society of the time. Probably of all these
stories we know best the Daphnis and Chloe of Longus,
which is of more historical interest because it is so nearly al-
lied to the pastoral romance of the age of Louis the Four-
teenth. The Latin Romance is illustrated in the Golden Ass
of Apuleius, which sets forth in fable a process of return from
sin into purity of life—it contains the beautiful episode of
Cupid and Psyche, and shows perhaps the highest art form
which the early romance exhibits.

The immediate source of the Romance of the Middle Ages
is in much dispute and probably it is not to be at all regarded
as a direct importation. Its elements are derived from various languages; these elements the spirit of the time grasps
and incorporates into a new whole. So, founded on the literature of other nations and introducing under various guises
different heroes of Gothic, Saracen and Classic Mythology,
the Mediæval Romance is still to be considered as the outgrowth of its age—an age when the Feudal System was yet
established and when Chivalry was at its height. The incon-
gruities of the time, its ignorance and consequent preju-
dice manifest themselves, for while man had certainly learned
that he was something other than his corporeal substance, he
had yet arrived at no real recognition of his spiritual self.
Of these Romances there seem to be two classes, to the
Northern and purer of which belong the Story of Arthur and
the Knights of the Round Table from the history of Geoffrey

of Monmouth, and those other chronicles which have Charlemagne for their hero. These narrate the adventures of Knights
who sworn to loyalty and truth are eager for adventure. The
basis of story is usually historical. Kings are introduced
into them but it is the Knight who holds in his hand the
thread of the story; who with power superior to that of his
feudal lord wanders in quest of adventures. It is now Arthur's Knights who kill the giants and out-wit the enchant-
ers; it is now Charlemagne's Paladins who vanquish the ogres
and destroy the emissaries of the invisible world. Neither in
its representative nor in its subordinate fictions however is to
be found the moral tone which might naturally be looked for
in the age of a purity professedly so great; obligations of
honor and regard for the sancity of human life are of as little
recognized power in literature as they are of real power in
society, yet modernized in diction and clothed with the garb
of poesy these stories are of interest as deep to-day as five
hundred years ago, and Arthur healed in the island valleys of
Avilion of his grievous hurts has in fulfillment of prophecy
reunited the " Table Round."

The Southern form of the Middle Age Romance as shown
in Amadis de Gaul differs little from the type just alluded to,
except that it deals rather with gallantry than with chivalry
and that its moral tone is lower. With its cotemporary of
Italy it may, however, be regarded justly as one of the store-
houses of our literature, since to it both Sidney and Shakespeare owe characters as well as incidents. In the Gesta
Romanorum, a curious compound of classical and of Rabbini-
cal lore, Gower and Chaucer as well as our great dramatist,
together with many authors of less repute find subject and,
perhaps, in a degree, inspiration. To it the later Italian writers, notably Boccaccio, are under direct obligation, and we
through them, for the Decameron has furnished to Shake-

speare the plots of Cymbeline, of 'All's Well That Ends Well,' if not for other plays, while Chaucer's Canterbury Tales are constructed upon its plan and owe to it some, at least, of their material. In short the Decameron of Boccaccio has had upon our literature a remarkably strong influence. The first English translation, incomplete, however, and supplemented by a second volume soon became very popular and gave direction, perhaps expression, to the public taste even where it failed to produce direct imitation.

The spiritual gloom of the dark ages as well as their intellectual blindness made it necessary that the truths of religion as understood by the monks should be presented in some readily appreciable form, and the same causes which led the church to the adoption of the Mysteries had influenced it at a somewhat earlier time to set forth in pious fable the lives of the Saints, the miraculous interpositions of Providence on behalf of persecuted innocence, the dire temptations of malign spirits, the final triumph of the just through the medium of the *Vies des Peres* or the Legenda Aurea.

At a later period out of the tales of the Trouvères and Troubadours grew, naturally, the fiction peculiar to the times of Louis XIV. and of his immediate predecessors. The spiritual element which has been incorporated into the literature of the Middle Ages disappears, and prose fiction attempts a return to the pastoral style of a much earlier time. Its ultimate aim seems, however, to be merely the portrayal of the vagaries of the court-life of the period—its beauties and defects may all be found in the Arcadia of Sir Philip Sidney, a work of genius truly, yet disfigured by extra poetic license and by Italian conceits of style. Out of this revived pastoral grows a new school which, founded like its predecessor on classic models, prefers to the Bucolic Era the Heroic Age and in which many features of the Romance of Chivalry are retained. Attacked by Moliere in 1659 this school was effectually shaken by Les Heros de Roman of Boileau and at the beginning of the 18th century had lost almost wholly its prestige; its visionary characters and unreal issues were as powerless before the weapons of satire as had been the Soldans and Paladins of Chivalry when attacked by the sword-like pen of Rabelais, of Cervantes or of Le Sage.

There survived a class of works in which we recognize the prophetic forerunners of the modern novel, of this class the Princess of Cleves may be taken as representative; while this work has claim to historical value as a faithful transcript of the time, its essential worth lies in this, that it deals with real human nature and recognizes the real issues of human life; influenced of course by the false sentiment of the earlier time and faculty in many particulars, it yet marks the transition to an age of reason—a transition the more remarkable since it occurs in an era when the splendors of the Grand Monarch's Court had so dazzled the world that magnificent vice seemed indistinguishable from rigid virtue.

If imaginative writing gives final utterance to the fears, the questionings, the aspirations of the soul of man, it may be possible to trace some connexion between the development of . fictitious literature and the growth of the world's thought. Going back to the Romance of Chivalry or still farther, we find the idea of the purpose of life, or the religious idea, to consist merely in this, that man created he knows not for what, beholding the coming and going of human life according to no purpose that he can recognize, stands awe-struck by a power he can neither comprehend nor withstand and believes himself the plaything of the Fates—the creature of gods benevolent or malignant who speak to him in the wind or in the storm. So we discover a hero whose efforts hardly even directed by himself are constantly thwarted by interpo-

sition of supernatural p███████at a later period man becomes
better informed and begins, in some degree, to feel though not
to recognize his freedom; now we have the stories of Chivalry,
and now it is for a personal Deity whose earthly kingdom is
to be established that the Knights go forth. The reaction
against that oppression and degradation of the poor which
was so natural a consequence of the Feudal System, is evidence of a higher idea of the purpose of life, if it be not the
first acknowledgment that life has a purpose at all. Man had
too long felt himself the creature of the mythologic gods, however, wholly to renounce them even now ; his difficulties and
dangers, his triumphs too, must needs present themselves
in an objective form ; he could not yet realize the purely
spiritual. Still in this transition state man proves his
instinctive fealty to one living and true God, since genii
and magicians, giants and dwarfs, enchanted castles and
labyrinths, alike vanish at the shadow of the cross. Later stories mark various periods of transition, of action and
reaction, and exhibit the peculiarities incident to phases of
civilization when great magnificence on the one hand is set
over against miserable squalor on the other. Such epochs
are characterized by the absence of any rational idea of the
value of life prevading all classes and tending to unite
in sympathy the rich and poor; a superficial elegance dwelling forever on some imagined field of the Cloth of Gold ig-
nores all interests which do not pertain to its feudal aris-
tocracy, and manifests little more knowledge of the human
heart, out of which the Apostle tells us are the issues of life,
than does the Ephemera of the material world in which its
brief day of existence waxes and wanes.

But time moved on ; the influence of the great poets and of
the great philosophers went abroad ; the whole nation sought
expression and found it at last in the novelists.

As the chosen art form of ███ literature of the Nineteenth Century modern fiction presents some curious problems not least of which is that it has superseded if not dethroned the drama. Adopted by classic states when the vigor of their intellectual prime had perished, attempting vainly in the Mediæval ages to reconcile the external to the ideal; this species of literary effort has in our century absorbed into itself all other forms. From it as the fountain of the best thought, young and old draw knowledge; in it they satisfiy their longings for the good, the true and the beautiful; it holds "as t'were the mirror up to nature" shows "virtue her own feature, scorn her own image and the very age and body of the time his form and presence."

The introduction of movable scenery is said by Collier to give date to the decline of the drama, but in itself it is of course nothing more than an indication of change in popular taste consequent upon decay of imaginative power. When it becomes necessary unduly to exalt accessories the essential is already declining, and as the essential disappears the art form dies while its spirit seeks elsewhere for dwelling and expression. Thus by a strange metempsychosis, the soul of the drama entered the body of the Romance which had long been parted from spirit, and thenceforward if we have little true art on the stage we have notably true art in fiction.

The more we investigate the conditions under which we live the more does the novel of the Nineteenth Century seem to owe its origin to a real fitness of things, and to be almost of necessity the one expression of this age. The life of the Sixteenth Century was necessarily more individual, in a certain sense, than the life of to-day; the scarcity of printed books and the absence of newspapers prevented any but the most interrupted interchange of opinion among people in the lower ranks of life, while the great intellectual awakening of the nation had as yet taken her shape nor organization. When the people of this age, touched as they were by the new influence of thought and agitated by impulses which they could not analyze, saw the plays of Shakespeare represented on the stage of the Blackfriars or the Globe, they found an avenue of escape for their emotions in dramatic presentation; its intensity, its vividness, its action, the passion of their natures demanded. We less emotional and more critical, with infinitely greater means of education and self-development, care less for action and more for motive; having grown into reverence for man we have grown also into habits of intro-spection, and we try that which is presented objectively in literature by appeals to our own inner consciousness. What we are to enjoy then must be kept before us long enough to admit of study and of reflection; it is to be a perfect whole as the Tragedy is, but it will involve greater elaboration of de-tail—a more careful working out of parts.

Essentially the novel is dramatic, though it by no means follows that that is the best novel which can most easily be adapted to the stage. The novel diverges from dramatic re-quirements, however, in several important respects: Goethe says of it as distinguished from the drama, that "sentiments and events in the one are to be set over against character and deeds in the other." The sentiment of the hero by some means or another must restrain the tendency of the whole to unfold itself and to conclude. The drama on the other hand must hasten and the character of the hero must press forward to the end; it does not restrain but is restrained."

The novel certainly allows as the drama does not allow the emphasis of the subjective and in this sense may be said to be restrained in its development by the sentiments of the hero, and this the more truly if it attempt to set forth the theory of life and to reflect the human spirit as eminently does

Goethe himself in Wilhelm ⬤ ter, or as does George Sand in Consuelo. The process of spiritual growth cannot take place rapidly; it cannot be delineated rapidly. The emphasis of the subjective is characteristic of our time, which with all its restlessness has yet leisure to analyze its emotions and its thought. Very happy is it if its attention be directed but to the natural and healthy. Our representative poetry is the lyric; our representative prose is the novel. This latter shows not perhaps the actual collision of the drama, yet distinguishes agent from instrument, portrays the conflict of individual character and will with other individual character and will as well as with circumstances, furthermore it sets forth the conditions under which the represented action becomes possible.

Of the element of chance Goethe says that while some scope may be allowed to it, it must yet always be led and guided by the sentiments of the personages. "Chance may be pathetic," but "Fate" he says "ought always to be terrible." Goethe says further, "The novel hero must not be in a high degree active"—not so highly active, he means perhaps, that the action may not be temporarily suspended and naturally resumed without the interposition of an actual barrier to progress, otherwise there would be little opportunity for digression or for explanation, and action would tend in better books than those of Wilkie Collins to become the end as well as the means and thus to destroy the true aim of art which is the representation of the ideal in its totality—action not lost sight of, yet rather the means by which the inner spiritual life of the characters is to be translated into the world's language, than that which in and for itself has independent value, since no more in the novel than elsewhere is art released from its aim of representing in appreciable form that which is divine.

The characters of the novel have less than those of the drama the office of exciting pity and terror, but they must none the less be real people, not incarnated single ideas. It would not of course be false art to represent a dominant power of passion or principle, but with this must be combined all those other often contradictory motives, feelings, passions and aims, which make of each individual a complex whole—a being capable of diverse development and of diverse influence. From the unity in complexity of these characters the story must logically proceed. Since the range of the novelist in the choice of subject is very wide his choice of character will also be much more free from restraint that is that of the dramatist; he is, as above stated, only under obligation to show in what way any person of a certain represented character would naturally act—to tell us general truth in particular form. This he may do with as much or as little use of dialogue as he pleases, but he is bound to give us characters not mere word pictures. He may enter upon the scene in his own character when the action needs temporary support, and may describe and explain when the exigencies of the story require; his management of his appearances will often determine to what degree he possesses artistic insight. Probably it would not be far wrong to say, as some have done in the conclusion of this parallel, that the relation of the novel to the drama is, so far as external art form goes, similar to that in which painting stands to sculpture. The painting has the greater capability; it shows form indeed but adds thereto the phases of appearance, perspective, color, light and shade. The accessories and conditions of action so far as they are moral, the drama cannot represent directly, they must be reached inferentially; the cause must be found from its effect. What the novel loses in vividness it gains in power of self-interpretation.

We have discovered in education and in practical business many royal roads; our ascent of the Hill Difficulty has been so often aided that despite our habit of introspection we have grown into a state of semi-dependence. Everything is done for us and we expect to have it done no less in our ideal than in our real world, no less in our books that in our lives. We do not wish to discover for ourselves why those things which the novelist sets forth are true; we ask that he teach us these things one by one. We are grown more reticent too if we feel as keenly as did the people of Elizabeth's time, we have learned to be silent—a few tears, a season of despair and after each great sorrow we take up anew the burden of life. In our own utterance we have no relief from pain, but in our books the spirit in its "midmost heart of grief clasps secret joy." In our books too we find expression for those sentiments and emotions which pervading our minds and becoming part of our natures have yet never been framed in words. "To know how to say what other people only think, is what makes men poets and sages;" the true novelist is poet and sage in one. We have said that in literature our age demands interpretation; so it prefers the novel to the drama again because by this choice it is spared the necessity of translating the universal into its particular and of transporting characters from the dimness and distance of dramatic eras to the full light of its to-day, in which alone it is able to discern truth, in which alone it so identifies itself with the action as to feel pity or terror. The novel much more immediately than the drama holds for this generation a magic mirror in which man sees reflected his own image and in which he sees represented the possible future of his earthly life. The more realistic in its treatment the novel is the better up to a certain point it becomes, but it will deserve to lose in interest whenever it allows its fondness for realism to lead it into the attempt to elevate the essentially commonplace to the rank of art, that is to say when it becomes a mere transcript of sordid life in its external aspects, when it becomes photography not creative art; but it may find its material in any sphere of life or of nature if only it be pervaded by the free spirit of artistic truth. Our last great novelist has said: "Depend upon it you would gain unspeakably if you would learn with me to see some of the poetry and the pathos, the tragedy and the comedy, lying in the experience of a human soul that looks out through dull gray eyes and that speaks in a voice of quite ordinary tones;" and further, "Let us always have men ready to give the loving pains of a life to the faithful representing of commonplace things, men who see beauty in these commonplace things and delight in showing how kindly the light of heaven falls upon them."

Thus far we have spoken of the novel in its historical and psychological aspects; we turn now to the application of our principles of criticism to the modern fiction as illustrated in the works of some of the great novelists.

De Foe is properly to be regarded in order of time the first writer of novels; his works, of which Robinson Crusoe is the best known though perhaps not the most excellent, are removed very far from the Romance of Chivalry. The hero differs in no important particulars from ordinary men; he makes their mistakes, falls into their errors, and in all but career is their prototype; his adventures though wonderful are by no means improbable; given the situation and they follow logically. Constantly surprised we are as constantly reminded that our surprise has been quite naturally led up to. In style De Foe has some of the qualities of Bunyan, his words are the simplest and he indulges in no reflections; he has a story to tell which he thinks will commend itself, this story he tells with no words that are useless, yet with definite-

ness, with picturesqueness, with such minuteness of detail
that the illusion is perfect; it is for no imaginary being we
fear and tremble but for a real man on a real island suffering
real distress. Robinson Crusoe and his man Friday are more
real to us than is the man who lives in the next street. Yet
if the office of the novel be to deal with the deeper problems
of life, to show the reciprocal influence of character and to
set forth the triumphs of human freedom over circumstance,
then the writings of De Foe fail of true art value in so far as
they exhibit life only in its latter phase. Where so few characters are introduced it is impossible to delineate perfectly
even those attempted. No character can stand fully revealed
till it has been brought into contact, not with matter alone,
with the mere external conditions of existence, but with the
internal and spiritual as it exists in the mental life of other
human beings. A plot determined by circumstances alone
affords little opportunity for development of any such complexity of purpose or of interests as results when man becomes a member of society—the element of chance is much
too large.

Richardson patiently, subtly, and very gradually unfolds
character, so gradually indeed that minuteness grows weari-
some. The elaboration is however essential to the story as it
exists in the author's mind. By almost inperceptible touches
he reveals to us the characters whom we follow hardly conscious whither we shall go; arrived at the end of the book, at
last we discover how all the apparent obstacles to progress
were really helps to the denouement. Pathos which touches
the outer edge of pain, vibrates through these books, yet is
the result of purely natural causes and we prove that the
pleasure of expectation is indeed higher than that of surprise.
The circumstances are no longer mere accidents; they are the
limitations of other minds as well. The collision of charac-

ter with character, of character with society, begins to be portrayed—all this is especially true of Clarissa Harlowe which we take as representative. Richardson's chief fault apart from the prolixity incident to his method is an evident eagerness to point a moral. Not so Fielding. More than almost any other of our prose authors is his method that of Shakespeare, and more than almost any other writer of the Eighteenth Century may he lay claim to the birthright of genius. What his characters do, they do from the inherent force of their natures, their acts and words are the legitimate outgrowth of themselves, acts and words alike deduced logically from the character, not by the most casual observation to be mistaken for the deeds and words of any other. The individuals selected are not from any peculiar fitness subjects of attention; neither Tom Jones, nor Sophy, nor Squire Western is in any way remarkable, but they are all imbued with a most human interest, and while thoroughly individual are yet types of the classes which they represent. Combined with this profound method in the portrayal of manners is an equally profound skill in the development of the plot. The succession of events constantly surprises us, and as constantly we see that we had no occasion whatever for surprise, since effect merely follows efficient cause. Fielding's faults glaring as they no doubt are, are those of his age, an age of the greatest coarseness of expression known to our literature—the interregnum between the Age of Chivalry and the dawn of modern opinion and thought. Fielding's justice is the true poetic justice, man is painted as he is, such as nature and his time have made him, but to him all the consequences of his deeds return. Yet Fielding's characters are after all more nearly the characters of the Drama than of the novel, that is to say they are in a measure isolated, their lives work out from within almost unrestrainedly; they make their

own world and are not sufficiently passive to meet the require-
ment which Goethe makes of the novel hero.

Other writers have illustrated various phases of fiction.
Sterne differs from Fielding as widely as may be in constructive
power; his story is a mere thread where that author's is a
perfect whole, yet a few of his characters are wonderfully
persistent, as too are some of Goldsmith's. Uncle Toby and the
Vicar meet us everywhere in literature and with their gentle
humor furnish to our not over-joyful life perpetual delight.
Periods of peculiar sentiment and thought, though here and
there reflected in some of their phases by minor writers, find
at last the man who is fully to represent his age and to leave
its record to all subsequent time.

The publication in 1765 of Percy's Reliques roused throughout England the long dormant interest in our old ballad
poetry whose picturesque vigor and directness appealed anew
and most powerfully to the popular heart stirring its blood as
in an earlier day it had stirred Sidney's like the blast of a
trumpet. To this republication we no doubt owe the Waverly
novels. The Highlands of Scotland are fitly the abode of the
romantic and the wonderful; their legends were to the novelist an unwrought mine. Scott seems however to have been
affected by little true feeling for his work as art: Carlyle goes
so far as to say he regarded it merely as a trade, which is not
the truth of the matter exactly. What is true is, no doubt
this, that he found his work no end in itself, to be wrought
out with life-long devotion, but rather a means by which Abbotsford might be rehabilitated.

> " In the elder days of art
> 　　Builders wrought with greatest care
> Each minute and unseen part—
> 　　For the gods see everywhere."

Probably Scott was no builder of this kind; he wrote rapidly, rather, as it seems from his works, with an eye to effect than with conscientious effort to embody truth. His works show much attention to details in the merely external, but have few persistent or individual characters, and their plots are very imperfectly constructed, whenever their construction is his own. Scott is properly entitled to the honor of being regarded the founder of the modern historical novel of the romantic school, but to learn how much his best efforts may suffer when compared with the work of an artist it is only necessary to compare Ivanhoe with the Romola of George Eliot. Mr. Leslie Stephen, says, after recounting Lockhart's story of the carved oak in imitation at Abbotsford and of the coats of arms in stucco: "This anecdote gives the true secret of Scott's failures. The plaster looks as well as the carved oak for a time, but the day speedily comes when the sham crumbles into ashes, and Scott's knights and nobles like his carved cornices become dust in the next generation."

Dickens and Thackeray are realists in the most exaggerated sense of the term. Realism in representation seems indeed to be Dickens only ideal of art; but even this ideal he does not often attain since his efforts are constantly thwarted by the melodramatic tendencies of his own nature. He never seems to realize the fact that art dare not be as strange as truth sometimes shows itself, since its office is to represent under the guise of variety the constant and the fixed. It is much to be doubted if any true art can be found in Dickens, for his work seems throughout to be characterized by absence of comprehension of the unity and purpose of life. He depends more even than Scott upon plaster and stucco, except that his plaster and stucco but seldom serve such ornamental purposes as cornices and coats of arms. Dickens' art has for itself no lofty ideals, it has none for the reader. From the study of his works seems to come little love of duty for duty's sake. When one recalls to his mind Dickens' characters it is always the grotesquely caricatured who respond to the summons. Where he introduces, as he often does introduce, persons actuated by high motives and obedient to duty, they are too often overshadowed in the representation by characters, let us rather say caricatures, whose only claim to our attention is found in such external oddities and inherent peculiarities as would make them unendurable in real life. Yet you are fain to acknowledge Dickens' power; he plays on your heart-strings most subtly; he moves you at his will to laughter or to tears, while through it all and especially after it all you feel that you are unjustly dealt with and are conscious of the rousing in you of a species of resentment. Dickens' characters are never particular forms of the universal and as such eternal; they are sincere and true often from instinct, just as dogs are faithful; but of men or women walking intelligently in the path of duty for duty's sake there are few examples. There is much blind devotion, much generous impulse, much foible, much idiosyncrasy made flesh; but little reason, little return, in any true sense of action to its originator. There is everywhere revealed however that wonderful power which had only need of truth to render it immortal.

The objective method was inseparable from Thackeray's art, for the satirist proper finds little exercise for his gift when he descends to the springs of life and reaches the ultimate motives of action. He finds much to reflect upon, much to wonder at, much to pity and regret, but little to satirize; life at its fountains is so essentially tragic that but fairly to comprehend it paralyzes mirth. To his own idea of art Thackeray is, however, always true; an ardent admirer of Fielding he has something of his master's method together with much of his genius. His books have too the charm of being in

harmony with the man, tender to humanity if keen sighted to
its faults, and throwing their influence in their own way on
the side of the true and brave. Thackeray does not often
descend to minutiæ and seldom seems to explore the remote
causes of individual action; he sees these things all clearly
enough and drops a hint here and there which shows how
much or how little force he attaches to circumstance, yet he
remains throughout true to his profound conviction, that
what a man is when he enters upon the stage of life, this he
will always remain—if true, then true and brave to the latest
day of life—if false, then false and a coward to his grave. His
clear eyes look through its bodily guise into the world's heart,
and what he sees he writes, and if he nothing extenuates he
also sets down naught in malice.

On behalf of the novel of the strictly objective school it may
perhaps justly be said that it withstands the desire of the present age for explanation and elucidation properly; that if it
present a faithful portraiture of external life it pre-supposes
the conditions of that life, and that in this world itself in the
long run practical justice is meted out even if the mills of the
gods do grind but slowly. It may be urged too that it is better for a man's intellect that even against his will he be
obliged to determine the conditions of thought and the circumstances of character which render certain trains of action
possible to certain represented individuals. It would indeed
at first glance seem so, since it is certainly a fact that diligent
study of real life may bring to light the eternal laws which
govern human society; yet it is equally true that in most
cases the presuppositions of the character are not within
our cognizance, while the consequences of various modes of
life or of certain courses of action whether good or bad are
effectual not immediately nor in ways readily appreciable.
Had we even power to penetrate, for the moment, into the in-

most soul of man, had we power to find there the record of his past, the prophecy of his future, it would still happen through the complexity of human life that but seldom would a character remain sufficiently long under our observation to determine the accuracy of our judgment. It is in the soul that the real man dwells; it is in the spirit that the absolute of art resides. So in the novelist's work that seems to be the only true art which enters into the soul and shows how from the soul the outward life grows, which depicts the real issues of human existence and delineates those emotions and sentiments which are common to the men of all ages; yet it is to represent not classes but individual beings personally free and personally responsible; it is to trace the reflection of action upon character and to estimate the force of trivial incidents in the swerving of disposition or in determining the manifestations of temperamental peculiarities, and it is to show the uniformity and persistence of the laws of cause and effect—in so far as it accomplishes these ends it fulfills its office and becomes the most powerful moral instrument of our times.

Of novels dealing with the deepest problems of psychology, those of Hawthorne are perhaps most remarkable, the more especially since their style affords so good an illustration of the possible concordance of thought with its mode of communication, yet they deal rather with the exceptional than the general principles of life, and exhibit most profound acquaintance with the morbid in character rather than a sympathy with the natural and the healthy. They touch the grotesque, even the horrible, but the withholding power of genius has prevented any nearer approach to the modern sensational fiction of the French.

In George Eliot the truly psychological novel finds its

apotheosis; she has brought to her work the power to keep God's image in repute and dares

> "To look into the swarthiest face of things
> For God's sake who has made them."

Her knowledge of human nature is the innate knowledge of itself and of its compeers which has belonged to Shakespeare and perhaps to a few other minds of perfectly developed genius. She writes under a command like that of old: "Write the things that thou hast seen, the things which are and the things which shall be hereafter." She shows us the convergence of lives and of influences, solves better than any one else has done the problem how best to reconcile the persistence of character with the effect of those things external to the mind which have a bearing either direct or indirect on the manifestation of the individual life. Her world is as real as the world about us; her justice is the true artist's justice, not always offering tangible rewards to virtue, not always visiting open punishment on vice, but showing the inevitable tendency of the spiritual life toward the good through manifold weakness and failure, or to the evil even though in no direct violation of human law; she shows the cumulative force of circumstances, the collision of the individual with other individuals or with society; her solutions are the solutions of real life—of a life that would be meaningless and vain but for the soul's immortality.

We have devoted no time to foreign works since there seem to be few types not fully represented in our literature. The novel in its present form seems legitimately the outgrowth of the Anglo Saxon power of assimilation which is no less evident in its literature than in its language. Prose fiction has grown, as we have endeavored to show, very gradually yet very surely into fuller and freer life having in each of its stages met more nearly the requirements of the true artistic spirit. It has, in short, from inert matter become at last a living organism whose free spirit of art has been to us in the past for solace, rest and hope and which in the future shall as well

> " Uphold us, cherish, and have power to make
> Our noisy years seem moments in the being
> Of the eternal silence."

GRACE C. BIBB.

THE LAY OF THE WANDERER.

(*From the Elder Edda.*)

I. BALDER'S DREAMS.

To Asgard thronged the anxious gods in haste;
The stately goddesses their presence graced.
Grave was their purpose, and their question deep:
Why dreams of darkness haunted Balder's sleep !

Auspicious dreams no more to sweetness lull
The sleep of much loved Balder, beautiful!
They asked the götuns, who the future see,
If this forboded dire calamity.

And came the sad response, that unto death
Was Balder destined—he the dearest breath !
Odin and Friga were with sorrow quelled;
And the sad gods their solemn council held.

And they resolved each being to beseech
That Balder's life no harm should ever reach.
And every being swore his life to spare :
Friga received their oaths with gladness rare.

Odin, forboding still. is filled with dread
That Balder's Guardian Spirits all had fled!
The gods again in concourse he doth crave;
And much is then devised in council grave.

II. THE DESCENT OF ODIN.

And now the Lord of Men uprose, and bade
With saddle fleetest Sleipner to be clad;—
Downward to Niflheim* his gallop rang;
When forth from Hela's† gate a gaunt hound sprang!

Upon its nether jaw the blood was red,
And clots its slaughter-craving throat o'erspread,
Its horrid fangs at Odin snapped amain ;
And fearful howlings shook the dismal plain!

And quaked the earth beneath him as he rode!
But still he sped toward Hela's dark abode ;
Beside the eastern gate, in mist and gloom,
He paused and found the far-sought Vala's ‡ tomb.

And there he chanted dead men's awful tunes !
Northward he turned and laid the potent runes ;
Dark incantations muttered—spells to seek
The dead, and force her to arise and speak !

------

* The land of mist; the nethermost of the nine worlds.
† Hades; or the abode of Death.
‡ A prophetess.

VALA.

Who is the dauntless man on distant quest
Who rudely breaketh now my spirit's rest?
In snowy shroud, and drenched with icy rain,
My bones have long in Death's embraces lain!

ODIN.

I, Veltam's son, was WANDERER named at birth;
Tell me of Hela—thee I call from Earth!
That glittering board—for whom of honor old—
For whom those couches overlaid with gold?

VALA.

For Balder couches wait in Death's hall here;
A shield is o'er the mead-cup's festive cheer;—
The race of gods shall yield to anguish meek!
I will be silent: force hath made me speak!

ODIN.

Be not thou silent! I will question thee
Until I know the deepest mystery,
Of Balder, loved one! Who with malice rife—
Oh! who will Odin's son bereave of life?

VALA.

Höder shall hither send, in death-trance dull,
His glorious brother, Balder, beautiful—
Fated, the life of Odin's son shall seek!
I will be silent: force hath made me speak!

ODIN.

Be not thou silent! I will question thee
Until I know the deepest mystery.
Who will on Höder wreak a vengeance dread?
Who, Balder's slayer lay on Death's cold bed?

VALA.

Rinda shall bear a son in her far home;
His hands he will not lave, nor gold hair comb—
Ere one night old he will dire vengeance wreak!
I will be silent: force hath made me speak!

ODIN.

Be not thou silent! I will question deep:
Who are the maidens that will bitter weep,
And wildly unto Heaven their long veils cast?
Tell this! Thou shalt not sleep until thou hast!

VALA.

Oh!—Thou'rt no WANDERER! I behold thee now!
I knew thee ODIN!—Lord of Men art thou!

ODIN.

Thou'rt not a VALA of wise prophecy!—
Thou art the mother of fierce giants three!

VALA.

Ride homeward, Odin! Boast thy journey's quest!
For ne'er another shall disturb my rest,
Until—when Loke breaks loose his fetters all—
The fearful TWILIGHT OF THE GODS ⸹ shall fall!

MYRON B. BENTON.

SPRING SONG.

(*Translated from J. G. v. Salis.*)

VERDURE clothes again our meadows;
Flowers perfume both hill and dale;
Finches sing in keen, glad joyance,
Tenderly the nightingale.
All the tree-tops brighten greener,—
Cooing, wooing, fills the grove:
Every shepherd now grows bolder,
Shepherd maids incline to love.

⸹ Ragnaröck; the anticipated destruction of the Universe, including gods and men.

Blossoms from the bud unfolding
Spring unvails in leafy drifts,
Dyes the velvet of the primrose,
Silver powder o'er it sifts.
From their broad leaves springing beauteous
Lilies of the valley see
Yield themselves as modest flowerets
For the breast of purity.

On their tender stems are tulips
Nodding gaily, yellow, red,
With its loving vines the woodbine
Weaves a canopy o'erhead.
All the breezes, now grown milder,
Fan us with the breath of love;
Spring's delights and scenes of pleasure
Move whate'er such joys can move.

J. C. PICKARD.

TO JOHN THE BAPTIST
THE GIVER OF UTTERANCE.

THIS famous hymn was composed by Paulus Diaconus, a Lombard monk of the 8th century. The initial sylla- bles of the verses in the first stanza are said to have suggest- ed to Guido Aretinus the names of the seven notes of his mu- sical scale, *ut* having been since changed to *do* for obvious reasons. Weitzius laments the idolatrous use of this hymn as a charm to recover the voice, singers appealing to John as their " tutelaris Deus."

The first stanza of the original is appended with a translation of the whole. The first chapter of Luke's Gospel will furnish sufficient commentary.

I.

Ut queant laxis
*Re*sonare fibris
*Mi*ra gestorum
*Fa*muli tuorum
*So*lve reatum
*La*bii polluti
Sancte Iohannes!

I.

Do thou O John divine
*Re*store thy servant's power to praise
*Mi*rific deeds of thine.
Far-sounding let our voices raise
*So*lfeggios sublime.
Lave clean our sin-stained lips, that lays
*Si*dereal may chime.

II.

From high Olympus forth
A messenger divinely sent
Foretold thy wondrous birth
And life in earnest labor spent.
Announcing too thy name
With prophecy of fame
He soothed the father's discontent.

III.

He, doubtful of the truth
Of heavenly promise thus revealed
And hope of faded youth,
Was stricken dumb, his mouth was sealed.
But thou didst form anew
With modulation true
The organs of the voice congealed.

IV.

Reclining in the womb
With piercing eye and joy elate
Thou sawest through the gloom
Thy King in bridal chamber wait.
By merit of their son
Each parent power won
Deep plans divine to penetrate.

V.

All praise to Sire above
All honor to begotten Son,
And to the holy Dove,
In sancity the paragon.
In every age and clime
Through everlasting time
The one triune, the triune one.

GEO. B. MacLELLAN.

THE SPHINX: A SONNET.

GREY with the dust of buried centuries,
  Scattered from Time's swift chariot-wheels along
  The silent ages, but still wise and strong,
An infinite grief in thine inscrutable eyes,
Thou sittest among thy mouldering memories;
  Making thee friends of the innumerous throng
  That lived and vanished, as a lofty song
Fills the mute air with music, and so dies.
Among the nations shifting like the sand
Of thine own desert; in a single day
Giddy with power and lightly swept away;

Thou sittest in scorn of man's weak littleness,
Above earth's petty turmoil and distress;
Sternly serene and desolately grand.

WAYLAND S. HYATT.

------------•------------

DEVELOPMENT IN RELIGION.

THERE was a time when in the thoughts of men all events in nature and society were looked upon as isolated and exceptional, as supernatural and miraculous. The relation of cause to effect, so far as comprehended at all, was then a very limited one; the natural order was little understood. The element of wonder working was uncalculated. The possible transformation of chemical and social forces had not been thought of. Creation was a miracle, Geology was a record of cataclysm and convulsion. Man, all orders in the three kingdoms, sprang fixed, full-grown and perfect upon the earth at the fiat of God. Language likewise and law, come as a gift, without the laborious delay of long generations of rudimentary experiment, modification and development.

Religions, especially to all the people who accepted them, were at some epoch of history communicated entire as a divine revelation and theophany; in no sense depending upon the growth and expression of a common consciousness, need and aspiration among the people. The men who brought or or even taught these religions, were not supposed to have been born, or to have lived in the natural way. They were held to be as exceptional as the messages of which they were the medium; and all through their history they are distinguished from ordinary men by some signal manifestations of divine honor and power. Even their common acts are magnified into miracles, and at death they are translated or become gods or demigods, in the worship of the established faith. You may verify these facts by a study of any of the various world religions.

In a later period, and especially in our own, the exceptional ceases to be miraculous. We do not straightway make haste to say an event is supernatural because we do not just now understand it. *We suspend judgment* until further investigations. This is the characteristic of civilization and culture. Of course, we are still challenged by the shallow and unreflecting to decide at once, to give an answer at sight, concerning all strange phenomena. "If it isn't this and thus; what and how is it?" they cry, expecting you to be compelled to their view of the case. If this is not a special providence, a direct answer to prayer, a miraculous cure, a reappearance of the dead, a case of witchcraft, a warning and judgment of God—then what is it? But we are in no haste to affirm; on the whole we are rather disposed to doubt or deny. In any event we take further time for consideration, remembering how so many things are in time explained by natural causes; understanding now how all occurrences do depend upon certain previous processes of preparation; how every result small or great is in reality a development and growth, long preparing in the womb of time.

We look out upon society as it is, and we are immediately led to a contemplation of society as it was. A great accumulation of facts brought together by the student and man of science in these latter years takes us back into a history once undreamed of. Written history will take us back three or four thousand years, perhaps, and then we find the world of men

The Western.

MARCH, 1876.

Holland, F. A.

THE SOUL OF SHELLEY.

POETRY may be classified into two kinds which, while so intermingling as to allow no definite line of division, do yet, according to the predominance of either in his work, distinguish the genius of the poet. These two kinds are the observant and the speculative. The observant sees things as they appear, and has a certain power of interpretation in detecting semblances and contrasts invisible to the common view. The speculative searches behind appearances for their essential meaning, and in its wanderings of imagination would fain surprise Truth disrobed in her deepest haunt of mystery. Of the former, Homer is the greatest example among the ancients, and Shakespeare among moderns. Of the latter, Job sovereigns the old world of literature, and Dante, Milton, Goethe and—may I not say—Shelley, reign in the new.

Homer has no theories. Good and evil engage his attention by the incidents of their manifold strife, but raise no questionings of their origin or nature or destiny. His gods are simply men of extraordinary stature. He sees heaven and earth in the same plane of vision and all that they contain, vast and little, permanent and fleeting, with equal vividness of conception. In the rush of warring years not the nod of a helmet misses his glance, not the least device upon a shield, not the vibration of a bow-string, not the length of a warrior's stride, nor even the petty household-cares with which the wives of heroes busy their hearts from fear of evil tidings from the fray.

So too with Shakespeare, whose sight, broad and minute as Homer's, goes deeper into the mind. Where Homer sees a will vanquished by one conspicuous passion, Shakespeare sees it beset and borne down by a multitude. A single life furnishes him a field of Troy whereon a whole Iliad of motives struggles through plots, dissensions, delays, numerous assaults to its moral catastrophe. Yet describing it he does not take part—he only looks on in thought. No conjectures of the whence and how and whither of life distract the gaze which engrosses all his faculties and transforms them into a magnifying lens of such wondrous power that merest sporules of emotion, impalpable to the minds in which they lurk, are imaged by it large as full-grown deeds.

In Job we observe a different type of genius. His pictures of nature and man, sublime and tender as they are, beyond rivalry, compose the background of a study on which lie, like the shadows of the crosses in Gerome's painting of Golgotha, the dark crucial problems of the soul.

Likewise, Dante's dream, under its magic realism of scenery borrowed from earth and only changed to ghastlier or more gorgeous colors by being placed amid preternatural light, conceals a grave philosophy of religion—the work of outraged conscience, mournful pity and disappointed love, phrasing the universal knowledge of an epoch into an answer that may still their cry for justice, mercy and peace.

Milton's epic has for its central figure around which all others are grouped for illustration and relief, the strength, courage, and majesty of will, which, as divine attributes, rendering their possessor, though a fiend, God-like still in power of fascination, enable Evil to cope with the omnipotence of Good.

Goethe cannot be strictly designated either an observant or speculative poet. He is equally native to both regions. His intellect is planetary—takes all the lights and shadows of a diurnal round of experience and at the same time moves along an infinite orbit about the Unknown. The poem, however, in which he sought to give paramount expression of his, mind, belongs to the speculative order. Faust is an attempt to solve the riddle of the soul. The soul seeks happiness and finds misery; knowledge leads to doubt, not to certitude; superiority to one's fellows is elevation to a solitude without sympathy; virtue failing to compensate for the loss of pleasures renounced in pursuit of higher joy, seems a detestable cheat. In desperation now the soul makes a compact with the spirit of Evil, and surrendered to his guidance, ranges without scruple the entire realm of Sense and Action, but again misses the happiness it would find. Had it been only wise, it would have known at the beginning what is taught by the end of this career, that right to happiness it has none, nor even to existence; that being, it should content itself within the conditions of being, and as a river which may have acquiescent smoothness of flow but cannot by yearnful billows become an ocean, glide without fretting against its shores, in whatsoever channel Nature has left for its course.

To this princely line of poets I have ventured to add the name of Shelley. Such rank, in my judgment, he deserves, not only because of the promise of powers which never reached their ripest fulfillment, but also by virtue of achievements which, considered, independently of the youth of their author, are prodigies, and as the works of one so young, almost miraculous.

That his place has not yet been fixed in literature is due mainly to the anticipative character of his poetry which needed another era than his own to recognize its prophetic inspiration. Shelley was at war with society as he found it, and society could not repress its indignation enough to hear any music in his denunciations of its most cherished customs. What music it did hear was in the lyrics which descanted on congenial themes and which, because heard, compelled its praise as perfect. But these were the playful warblings of a genius that took rest in them for louder and more earnest tones of thought. To Shelley's contemporaries outspoken thought was discord. It grated upon their prejudices already nervous with fear of revolution, and they called it madness.

The singer's life they regarded as proof of this insanity, because the life corresponded with the song. How could a man be rational who defied public opinion? Did not the folly of such defiance demonstrate aberrancy of intellect? What was to be gained by it?—not wealth nor popularity nor high position. And who but a madman would challenge with vociferous rhyme public scrutiny to conduct which was altogether unprofitable and plainly hostile to self-interest? So Shelley's contemporaries reasoned and doubtless felt their anger subside into a sense of charity under the effort to mitigate by such excuses his crime of thinking.

Moreover at that time poetry was deemed to consist more in finish of form than in richness of material. Criticism had adopted canons as conventional as the manners of the court. A drama must have five acts—so verse must have a certain number of syllabic feet, a certain ratio of imagery to literalness of style, and a certain set of subjects exclusively dedicated to Art. Art could not be didactic. Art must not reason.

Art should not excite disagreeable emotions, as, for instance, by opposing prevalent beliefs. Art must keep her fair complexion from freckling with exposure to the rude air of politics, and cultivate in seclusion the toiletry of sentiment.

This method of criticism Shelley despised and said of it— " It sprang up in that torpid interval when poetry was not. It never presumed to assert an understanding of its own ; it has always, unlike true science, followed, not preceded, the opinion of mankind, and would even now bribe with worthless adulation some of our greatest poets to impose gratuitous fetters on their own imaginations and become unconscious accomplices in the daily murder of all genius either not so aspiring or not so fortunate as their own." He, for one, would not submit to its shackles. He set up the standard of revolt, and the revolt has since become a successful revolution. Melody is to be measured by accents, not by a thumb-rule. Imagination and Fancy may shine over a poem as the sun over the sea, and turn every rippling line to sparkles. Greece is a goodly land, and excursions to its groves and mountains pleasant enough for holidays of reminiscence, but men are alive now as truly as they were when Parnassus reached half-way to heaven, and the Now with its pangs of travail for a birth of better manhood, should inspire the singer's loftiest strain. So from the Present and the Future Shelley took his themes, or rather, the themes took possession of Shelley's spirit and with its voice of perfect melody told their story of pain and wrong, their hope of triumphant Right. Other poets were more or less skillful workers in verse and might observe the rules of their craft with advantage, but Shelley's soul was poetry itself and whatever passed through it became a poem. Artist he scarcely can be called. Critical as was his intellect, its faculties of criticism were overborne by the mightier impulse of creation. Criticism

is the office of prose; it demands for its task the cooler
moods of thought, and when performed by the poet himself,
implies a limit to the creating power where the mind becomes
reflective by reaction. But limit Shelley's imagination seldom, if ever, reached. It could not pause long enough to
look calmly back on its course. Its very rests were lyric
pantings. Nought but the utmost stretch of words could
momentarily check its flight, and even they, while restraining,
were lifted, by its effort to transcend them, into meanings
strange because higher than their wont. In two days this
panurgic mind-force wrought a poem as long as one of Tennyson's Idyls of the King, and rich as any of them in jewels of
fancy well-set in metrical gold; in two months a tragedy
surpassed by none but Shakespeare's; in six months an epic
drama that vies with the life-time labors of the giant bards of
our race; and in five years ending before the thirtieth of the
poet's age was complete, a volume of verse which has proved
a mine of suggestions to succeeding poets such as Tennyson,
Browning, Arnold, Buchanan, the Rossetis and Swinburne, as
well as to our own Lowell, who more than any other has
caught the spirit of Shelley's Odes and inherited their wealth
of phrase at once philosophic and pictorial. Verily it was a
frenzy of song which had seized this minstrel and kept him
in perpetual transport of utterance. He had the genuine
madness of the muses, the Bacchic intoxication without which,
according to Plato, "Whoever approaches the poetical gates,
having persuaded himself that by art alone he may become
sufficiently a poet, will find in the end his own imperfection,
and see the poetry of his cold prudence vanish into nothing-
ness before the light of that which has sprung from divine
insanity."

Hence the rapt bard sang, albeit without hope of audience
from his own time—sang because his soul overflowed with

music pouring into it through every sense, and from all the air of thought. Audience he felt that he would have but from another age and that age already existed in his mind; for his was an ideal world where present and future are one. There his opinions were powers, his abstractions personalities, his hopes the very ground on which he walked and " an over-hanging day."

Shelley's idealism differed from that of the metaphysicians who hold theirs as a result of logical processes to have no influence on the ordinary life by whose instincts and duties it is contradicted. His conceptual faculty was too vivific to allow any inference to lie dead in its sight, and no sooner was the inert idea seen than it was under a warm embrace which made it live and become a part of the soul's own life. In no other poet has speculation been so intimately identified with feeling, desire, being itself. Other poets have first speculated and then translated their speculations into symbols of outward reality. But to Shelley their reality was the dream and their dream the reality. Instead of attempting to express thought in images of sense, it was more his effort to animate the things of sense with the most delicate traits of thought. In his mind the barrier between the inward and outward was broken down and they blended in a vague sentiment that was almost consciousness of another mind of which the two worlds were different and yet identical manifestations.

Here at last the Berkleyan Philosophy had found a genius native to its finest ether.

" Some truths there are ," wrote Berkley, " so near and obvious to the mind that a man needs only open his eyes to see them. Such I take this one to be, viz., that all the choir of heaven and furniture of the earth—in a word, all those bodies which compose the mighty frame of the world—have not any substance without a mind ; that their being is to be perceived or known; that consequently as long as they are not actually perceived by me or do not exist in my mind, or that of any other created spirit, they must either have no existence at all, or subsist in the mind of some eternal spirit; it being perfectly unintelligible, and involving all the absurdity of abstraction to attribute to any single part of them an existence independent of a spirit." By the influence of this teaching Shelley's imagination was swept to cadences that ran as a sustaining undertone through all the varied measures of his music. So distinctly has he declared it in some of his strains that but for their tropical magnificence the words might be taken for an exact re-statement of Berkley's propositions, as when in Hellas, Ahasuerus says to Mahmud

"Sultan, talk no more
Of thee and me, the future and the past ;
But look on that which cannot change—the One,
The unborn and the undying.   Earth and Ocean,
Space, and the isles of life or light that gem
The sapphire floods of interstellar air,
This firmament pavilioned upon chaos,
With all its cressets of immortal fire,
Whose outwall, bastioned impregnably
Against the escape of boldest thoughts, repels them
As Colpe the Atlantic clouds—this whole
Of suns and worlds and men and beasts and flowers,
With all the silent or tempestuous workings
By which they have been, are, or cease to be,
Is but a vision ; all that it inherits
Are motes of a sick eye, bubbles and dreams.
Thought is its cradle and its grave ; nor less
The future and the past are idle shadows
Of thoughts eternal flight—they have no being ;
Nought is but that which feels itself to be."

Accordingly when Shelley looked out upon Nature, it was his own soul that he saw there—its moods, beliefs, fears and aspirations.   At one time

" 'The *gentleness of rain* is in the wind."

At another

" 'The grass sprung
Startled, and *glanced*, and *trembled*, even,
To *feel* an unaccustomed presence."

A woodland scene imaged in a pool

" Had lent
To the dark waters breast
Its every leaf and lineament
With more than truth expressed ;
Until an *envious* wind crept by,—
Like an unwelcome thought
Which from the mind's too faithful eye
Blots one dear image out."

Then there are scenes that partake of his own extreme
sense of the horrible, as when—

" Like a dying lady lean and pale
Who totters forth, wrapt in a gauzy veil
Out of her chamber, led by the insane
And feeble wanderings of her fading brain,
The moon arose up in the murky east
A white and shapeless mass."

At the death of Keats, all ' that he had loved and molded
into thought from shape and hue and odor and sweet sound,
lamented him '—

" Morning sought
Her Eastern watch-tower ; and her hair unbound
Wet with the tears which should adorn the ground,
Dimmed the aerial eyes that kindle day ;
Afar the melancholy thunder moaned,
Pale Ocean in unquiet slumber lay
And the wild winds flew round sobbing in their dismay."

Likewise, when Shelley's mind changed its view and looked
in upon itself, it found there a visible Nature. As sight
before had been thought, thought now became sight. He saw

'wintry forests' of grief, 'many-winding rivers' of reverie,
'light sands of consciousness paving the ocean of dreams,'
'drownings of sleep,'

> "Where the dreamer seems to be
> Weltering through eternity."

'moonlight of Love which hides the night of Dejection,'

> "From its own darkness, until all is bright
> Between the heaven and earth of the calm mind ;"

and long processions of personified mental attributes, as when
to mourn for Adonais

> "Desires and Adorations
> Winged Persuasions and veiled Destinies,
> Splendors and Glooms, and glimmering incarnations
> Of Hopes and Fears, and twilight Fantasies ;
> And Sorrow with her family of sighs,
> And Pleasure, blind with tears, led by the gleam
> Of her own dying smile instead of eyes
> Came in slow pomp ; the moving pomp might seem
> Like pageantry of mist on an autumnal stream."

Into this ideal world the poet had brought a sensitiveness
naturally excessive and irritated by the failure of visionary
experiments at mending the laws and institutions of his land.
Born under the star of the French Revolution, its fiery spell
was in his blood and fevered it to an almost hatred of oppression. At school he had resisted the brutal custom of
fagging and earned for himself a brave immunity. During
the few months of his residence at Oxford he had written to
well-known liberals with a design of organizing, if possible,
an association of reform—a small offense compared with the
villainy he afterwards perpetrated of presuming to use his
reason in matters of religion—villainy which was punished by
immediate expulsion from the privileges of the University.
Then the door of his father's house was shut against him,
his first love foreswore her troth, and the boy barely nineteen

years old betook himself to London in as desolate exile as if
he had been thrown on a South-sea island. But though fra-
gile the body that encased it, his was as dauntless a spirit as
ever informed the strength of a Titan. There were baronial
estates at home to which he was heir, but he preferred the
wretchedness of intellectual freedom. The pin-money of sisters at boarding-school near London, kept breath in his body
until his father consented with small annuities to let it stay
there; and a fair schoolmate who meanwhile had brought
their pittances to his hand, won its impulsive clasp in marriage. It was a marriage to be repented of—a chain upon the
very heart that vowed its energies to breaking the chains of
a race. These chains Shelley heard clanking everywhere—
iron on the feet of the poor to enslave them to a soil whose
harvests were not their own; gold on the wrists of the rich
who knew not that the bracelets they esteemed so pretty,
withheld their hands from worthier prizes; collars of unjust
law on the necks of whole peoples to drag them before
crowned apes of power, and visors of custom clamped over
the eyes of reason lest it should discover the absurdity of the
things it had been taught to reverence. Religion, too, seemed
to him a chain and its every rite and dogma links forged by
cunning priests to bind the homage of men to a despotism
enthroned in heaven as authority for all the oppressions of
earth. To break these chains and give man liberty, Shelley
believed, was to set him in the way of moral and social per-
fection. For man's vices, Shelley argued, were not innate but
the effect of adverse circumstances—of pernicious education.
All voluntary actions originated in opinions. Whatever man
did—of good or evil—he did because at the time he thought
it conducive to happiness. Experience would acquire wisdom
whenever left free to pursue it in all directions, alike through
folly and through prudence. The individual might perish in

the pitfall of his vices but humanity exists through many generations, and where one generation left off another would take up the career of training in a continuous progression towards a knowledge of right conduct, so full and clear and impressive as to constrain obedience to its directions. This philosophy of sagacious maxims and hopeful errors Shelley had learned from Godwin at whose feet he sat and who thus syllogized it in his Inquiry of Political Justice—

* There is no conduct in itself reasonable, which the refutation of error and dissipating of uncertainty will not make appear to be such. There is no conduct which can be shown to be reasonable, the reasons of which may not sooner or later be made impressive, irresistible and matter of habitual recollection. Lastly, there is no conduct the reasons of which are thus conclusive and thus communicated, which will not infallibly and uniformly be adopted by the man to whom they are communicated."

It was easy for Shelley to fill out and enforce this reasoning with illustrations which, though at first glance appearing refutatory, would on further examination change to proofs. What chiefly retards the progress of the species, he would say, and keeps it in chronic puerility is a system of government inimical to growth because growth threatens to overthrow it. As a part of this policy of dwarfage men are educated to lie and believe in lies. The bauble that glitters in the hand of a king is a lie. The king himself tricked up in meritricious dignity is a lie; and those who smirk, nod and kneel in masquerade of homage about his throne are still meaner lies ; while every path of service which leads to that high court of pretense rises rank by rank up a steep ascent of turpitude in lying. The jurisprudence that allows the lordling a thousand acres and kills the pauper who poaches on one of them, is but a chartered lie. The judge who distributes justice by classes the perjured arbiter of lies ; and every field of

---

* Pol. In. Vol. 1, Page 51, 2d Edition.

blood shed as the patriotic right of a government which wages war for a freak named honor and then grinds with poor laws the surviving families of those who fall in its defense, a lie so inexcusable and atrocious that the very elements are guilty in not combining with rage to forbid it. Nay more! Are there not upon the statute-books enactments which say "Thou shalt lie and swear that thy lie is truth?" Dare a man's mouth betray his inmost conviction? What if he should call the Prince-Regent a rake? How long could he claim as an indefeasible right equal privileges with the rest of his kind, and remain out of prison? Is it possible, then, for him to be true to himself—not to speak of his fellows—when with every breath he inhales hypocrisy and at every turn touches a fraud?

> " Oh that the wise from their bright minds would kindle
> Such lamps within the dome of this dim world
> That the pale name of Priest might shrink and dwindle
> Into the hell from which it first was hurled,
> A scoff of impious pride from fiends impure!
> Till human thoughts might kneel alone,
> Each before the judgment-throne
> Of its own aweless soul, or of the Power Unknown.
> Oh that the words which make the thoughts obscure
> From which they spring, as clouds of glimmering dew
> From a white lake blot heaven's blue portraiture,
> Were stripped of their thin masks and various hue,
> And frowns and smiles and splendors not their own,
> Till in the nakedness of false and true
> They stand before their lord, each to receive its due ! "
>
> —(*Ode to Liberty.*)

To liberty therefore which meant equality, sincerity, self-respect, generous emulation of noble examples and eagerness of culture—forces of social advancement which in co-operation would be irresistible—Shelley devoted his life. For three years the outlawed boy roved in a knight-errant's quest for exploits which should extend the fame of his mistress and show himself worthy to wear her arms on his escutcheon. Now he was in London and anon in Edinburgh; at York to-day, at Keswick to-morrow; this month in Dublin, the next at Nan Gwylt and afterwards in rapid transition at Radnorshire, Leynmouth, London again, Tanyrolt and Bracknell; writing pamphlets and letters, making speeches, trying to organize societies, always in debt because always giving his money to others less needy than himself, building dykes to save the houses of the poor from floods, studying medicine in hospitals to relieve the ailments of the poor without the charges that frayed almost to breaking the thread of wages that at best only kept them suspended over starvation, and finally contracting in his enterprise of charity an opthalmia which turned the beauty he most loved, to torture, as the very grass blades and boughs of trees cut themselves 'with microscopic distinctness' on his eyes.

But the notablest deed of this dream-haunted vagrancy was the letter to Lord Ellenborough. It was a veritable *deed.* Its words raug against intolerance like blows of a battle-axe —and their echoes are still abroad. Lord Ellenborough had passed a severe sentence on one Eaton, a bookseller, for publishing the third part of Paine's Age of Reason. The sentence roused Shelley's indignation. He was a mere stripling—not more than twenty years of age—but he denounced the outrage with invective worthy of the maturest intellect of Burke.

"What end," he asks, "is persecution designed to answer? Can it convince him whom it injures? Can it prove to the people the falsehood of his opinious? It may make him a hypocrite and them cowards; but bad means can promote no good end. The unprejudiced mind looks with suspicion on a doctrine that needs the sustaining hand of power.**** But I will demand if that man is not rather entitled to the respect than the discountenance of society, who, by disputing a received doctrine either proves its falsehood and inutility (thereby aiming at the abolition of what is false and useless) or gives to its adherents an opportunity of establishing its excellence and truth. Surely the individual who devotes his time to fearless and unrestricted inquiry into the grand questions arising out of our moral nature ought rather to receive the patronage than encounter the vengeance of an enlightened legislature. I would have you to know, my lord, that fetters of iron cannot bind or subdue the soul of virtue. From the damps and solitude of its dungeon it ascends, free and undaunted, whither thine, from the pompous seat of judgment dare not soar."

Increasing years bring wisdom, and Shelley soon ceased to look for any immediate result from his schemes of reform. Men had been too long in bondage to know the value of freedom. They were reconciled to their degradation and oblivious of its shame. Only when hungry would they growl and then a toss of meat would stop their mouths. Liberty could not be thrust upon them—it must be a desire before it can become a heritage. Time would have to work; segregated thinkers mewing their hope in secret, meet together; thoughts add themselves to thoughts until they should marshall and fly abroad in unseen troops of influence; theories, repulsive on account of their novelty, acquire by degrees the fascination of familiarity, and entering the unoccupied minds of a fresh generation, fashion them to more virile forms of character, before a nation could rise and stand in complete enfranchisement.

But, however long delayed, the day was sure to come. Shelley had the earnest of it in his own great hope, and the expanding prevision of dangers and difficulties in the way of its approach only sublimed his courage to encounter and remove them. But the strength to *do* was spent. His frail body was pining in consumption, his sympathies had grown so morbid that they suffered every pain they saw or heard of, and worst of all, a canker gnawed incessantly his heart—grief at the disgrace and suicide of his first wife, and at the loss of his children whom the law had wrested from him as unfitted by immoralities of opinion to be their custodian.

He cannot breast the tempest any more. Away in some friendlier clime he will seek a nest woven by Nature of hills and woods and streams for wounded spirits like his own. There forgetting the passions which prompt the lays of other poets but which for him to remember is to bleed afresh, he will sing in the world's night of its golden dawn. Dear as ever are the old themes—truth, freedom, the brotherhood of the race and its perfectibility—but now that he can bear no more the brunt of opposition in their service, the ear which would not listen to his ephemeral speech, shall hear them chanted in immortal psalms.

Nature welcomed him to her Italian solitudes as a pet child, and in their depths his aching head lay at rest as between the breasts of a great Mother. One can almost see a faun in the naked revels he has described himself as taking alone in a ravine near the Baths of Leucca—

"In the middle of the day, I bathe in a pool or fountain, formed in the middle of the forests by a torrent. It is surrounded on all sides by precipitous rocks, and the waterfall of the stream which forms it falls into it on one side with perpetual dashing. Close to it on the top of the rocks are alders and above the great chestnut trees, whose long and pointed leaves pierce the deep blue sky in strong relief. The water of this pool which, to venture an unrythmical paraphrase, is sixteen feet long and ten feet wide, is as transparent as the air, so that the stones and sand at the bottom seem, as it were, trembling in the light of noon-day. It is exceedingly cold also. My custom is to undress and sit on the rocks, reading Herodotus, until the perspiration has subsided, and then to leap from the edge of the rock into this fountain—a practice in hot weather exceedingly refreshing. This torrent is composed, as it were, of a succession of pools and waterfalls, up which I sometimes amuse myself by climbing when I bathe, and receiving the spray all over my body, whilst I clamber the moist crags with difficulty." —(*Letters to Peacock. Fraser's Mag.*, *March*, 1860.)

Shelley's love of nature was unique. Admiration the dullest sensibility feels when confronted by her grander aspects, and there is a kind of technical interest often mistaken for affection, which even among poets regards her less as a sovereign joy than as a model posing for pictures of phrase; but Shelley's love was a positive entrancement, a total eclipse of self by her closer presence on his soul. When he went to the woods it was not to hunt for a sonnet, nor when climbing mountains did he think of getting from their peaks a fine effect of sunset tints for inchoate cantos; he sought Nature solely from love, and that he might feel love's divinest thrill in contact with her beauty. Yet he knew by name and with recognition that was almost mutual, every tree and shrub and wild flower that grew in his favorite resorts—how the branches rambled from the trunk and were mimicked by the veins of the leaves, how restlessly the vines climbed and under what serpentine hues of blossom, how the sod ' scarce heaved when the tender blue-bell was born ' and the water-lily glowed with moonlight beams of its own, and the daffodil wets

> " Its mother's face with heaven-collected tears
> When the low wind its playmate's voice it hears."

He knew as well the passions and caprices of the sea—its shallows and depths of color and the hours they reflect, the blackening of its waves in the wind, and the rainbowed spray of hope with which they die in sunshine, and from the faintest wrinklings of its surface could tell what purpose, yet unformed, of wrath or pleasure had begun to stir within its heart. These, and many secrets which Nature refuses to persistent inquiry, Shelley learned by the still content of lying in her arms and overhearing her talk in sleep. And he learned more—the most enamoured tones of her voice which, spoken to his own spirit and transfused through it into song, made him the most musical of poets. This pre-eminency has been disputed by a recent critic* in favor of Swinburne; but

---

* E. C. Steadman.

the difference between them is the difference between genius of inspiration and genius of skill. Swinburne is a musician of words, Shelley a born singer. Swinburne's excellence is technical brilliancy of variation, Shelley's is essential grace of tune. Swinburne's sonatas are masterly tricks of art, but the impression they make is too much one of surprise at their nimble overleaping of difficulties of versification, to leave the mind free for full enjoyment of their rhythm; Shelley's profuse strains are but the audible pulses of his thought, spontaneous, easy and versatile in modulation, ranging at will through all the compass of sound, and even when wild, wild without discord, like the melodious respiration of a mocking bird.

When Shelley lauds the skylark, his measures take its earth-scorning spring and rise with the gladness of its soaring strain. When describing the sympathetic sisters of the sensitive plant, his voice has the peal of hyacinthine bells—

> " So delicate, soft and intense
> It is felt like an odor within the sense."

And echoes as they recede among distant hills mock themselves in his cadences with " low, sweet, faint sounds like the farewell of ghosts."

But Shelley's love of Nature, while both a passion and an inspiration, had other moods in which it became worship. Nature to him was then an apparition of God. He glimpsed God in her splendors, heard God in her voices, fell at God's feet on her high altar-places. Though generally believed to have been an atheist and himself accepting the nickname in a temper of youthful bravado, atheist he never was after the brief fit of the Queen Mab period of his youth had passed. In that day every kind of opinion that denied the traditional definition of God received the same stigma of epithet. Only one idea of His character was tolerated as consistent with an acknowledgment of His existence, and that idea was the most crudely mechanical and anthropomorphic. God was either the absolute ' carpenter and chemist' of the universe or an august name for nothing. To suppose Nature co-eternal with Him was to set up a rival Deity or propose a degrading partnership. Before Nature began, He had filled an eternity of boundless void with infinite sleep, and then one day awoke, did a week's work and immediately sank back again into sleep unbroken until now, save when some part of the universal machinery has run wrong and required Him to put in a finger of miraculous repair or providential adjustment. To deny such fabrication and control of Nature by a Being whose personality was further defined as consisting of human idiosyncrasies monstrified to superhuman bulk, was pronounced Atheism. Shelley accepted the title, but while doing so, insisted that ' his negation must be understood solely to affect a creative Deity,' and that in his poetry it was ' the erroneous and degrading idea which men have conceived of a supreme being that was spoken against, not the Supreme Being itself.'

After all, when it is remembered that the God of every man's worship is but his own conception of God and must fall as immeasurably short of the whole truth as an infinite Unknown transcends human ability to conceive it; that as much of this Truth as cannot be conceived must remain inoperative upon intelligence and therefore upon character so far as intelligence supplies its motives and principles; that this conception itself grows with the growth of all knowledge, being one thing in the Fetichist, another in the Greek, another in the Jew, another in the Buddhist, another in the Moslem, another in the Christian, and as manifold among Christians as their differences of information and circumstantial bias; when it is remembered that every mind which adores at all, adores its own ideal of what is greatest and best and most satisfactory as a solution of the mystery of life and its surroundings—this railing accusation of infidelity from one fallible mind against another appears in its proper aspect as nothing more nor less than a charge of difference of ideal or, in other words, of inequality of knowledge and dissimilarity of mental organism. What right have I to say—what else than arrogance can I exhibit by saying—that you deny God because you deny my trivial notion of His Majesty, or that you blaspheme His name by describing my notion as grotesque. It is your own God, not another's, that you are to believe in, reverence, and obey; to Him, and Him alone, you stand or fall.

With no conception of Deity did Shelley quarrel as the prerogative of the intellect that entertained it; it was the claim of the conception to an autocratic sway over all other intellects, and the accompanying threat of vengeance should they refuse submission, which his reason and sense of justice and love of liberty alike resented.

> " What is that Power? Some moon-struck sophist stood
> Watching the shade from his own soul upthrown
> Fill heaven and darken earth, and in such mood
> The form he saw and worshiped was his own,
> His likeness in the world's vast mirror shown ;—
> And 'twere an innocent dream, but that a faith
> Nursed by fear's dew of poison grows thereon,
> And that men say that Power has chosen Death
> On all who scorn its laws to wreak immortal wrath."

Unwilling to submit his reason to the guesses of others, Shelley was as reluctant to yoke it with a tight hypothesis of his own. He held is belief as tentative and to be displaced by any theory of the origin and purport of the universe which could more clearly explain its mystery. That mystery, however, was too dark for swift rushes or sudden leaps of faith. Enough if he could stumble through bogging inquiries to any

footway of speculation, and along that footway towards the
dimmest promise of Light. Even a Will o' the Wisp were
kind should it lead him out of the morass of doubt to firmer
thinking. More than once did he repine and fall, and as one
utterly spent, give up his heart to sobs, but the sobs of *his*
heart were a *miserere* of more than earthly music to lull its
despair. Thus, metaphysician as well as poet, he groped
from a materialism black as perdition to the twilight of an
idealism which, if it erred, erred by what might be called an
excess of Divinity—that is by the denial of all other existence
than the Divine—as one who had lived in protracted night and
for the first time saw the dawn might believe the light to have
created the objects it only reveals and that those objects have
no other reality than its revelation.

In Shelley's creed mind alone existed, and that mind was
the Eternal. All others were but portions of it, phases of its
meditation, thoughts projected into an appearance of entity
by the necessary law of intelligence, which cannot reflect upon its thoughts without objectifying them to the reflecting
self. He wrote, in an unfinished Essay on Life,

"Nothing exists but as it is perceived. Pursuing the same thread
of reasoning, the existence of distinct individual minds, similar to
that which is employed in now questioning its own nature, is likewise found to be a delusion. Let it not be supposed that this doctrine conducts to the monstrous presumption that I, the person
who now, write and think am that one mind—I am but a portion of it.
The relations of things remain unchanged by whatever system. Yet
that the basis of things cannot be, as the popular philosophy alleges, mind,
is sufficiently evident. Mind, as far as we have any experience of its pro-
perties, (and beyond that experience how vain is argument!) cannot
create—it can only perceive."

Shelley, however, did not believe the universal mind to be
similar to the individual. The latter was marked by limitations which could not bound the former. Man's conscious-

ness was but the sense of limitation to his personality— a personality that to the absolute mind could be nothing more than one of its own ideas. As such, it would have the life of that mind and feel such life in the intuitions which are independent of the understanding, which cannot be dissolved by analysis or conceived of as other than necessary and eternal, which are most impressive when consciousness of individuality is least distinct as if their inflow were obliterating the sense of limitation and flooding the finititude of thought with the infinitude of feeling—intuitions of the True, the Beautiful, and the Good. All else was phenomenal, evanescent, illusory; these alone were real and enduring. Whatever opened the mind most amply to their entrance was of all things that appear, most essentially Divine. Wherever they had genialest play, God might be said to abide as in a Shekinah. To Shelley this key of inner opening and this sacred dwelling place were the property of Nature. Nature withdrew his thoughts from 'the hate, fear, disdain, envy, self-love and self-contempt' of mankind, and soothed the rankling of that barb of a broken arrow which nothing but Death could extract from his heart. Nature communicated to his life the spirit of her own—the spirit of an all-pervading Beauty that does not differ from Truth and Goodness, but is one with them and the same. How worshipful with trust and love and earnest pleading his invocation of her aid—

> " Spirit of Beauty, that dost consecrate
> With thine own hues all thou dost shine upon
> Of human thought or form, where art thou gone ?
> Why dost thou pass away and leave our state,
> This dim vast vale of tears, vacant and desolate ?—
> Ask why the sunlight not forever
> Weaves rainbows o'er yon mountain river :
> Why aught should fade and fail that once is shown ; .
> Why fear and dream and death and birth

Cast on the daylight of this earth
Such gloom; why man has such a scope
For love and hate, despondency and hope?

No voice from some sublimer world hath ever
To sage or poet these responses given :
Therefore the names of Demon, Ghost, and Heaven,
Remain the records of their vain endeavor ;
Frail spells whose uttered charm might not avail to sever
From all we hear and all we see,
Doubt, chance and mutability.
Thy light alone, like mist o'er mountains driven,
Or music by the night-wind sent
Through strings of some wild instrument,
Or moonlight on a midnight stream,
Gives grace and truth to life's unquiet dream.

* * * * * * * * * *
* * * * * * * * * *

The day becomes more solemn and serene
When noon is past ; there is a harmony
In Autumn, and a lustre in its sky,
Which through the Summer is not heard nor seen,
As if it could not be, as if it had not been.
Thus let thy power, which like the truth
Of Nature on my passive youth
Descended, to my onward life supply
Its calm—to one who worships thee
And every form containing thee,
Whom, Spirit fair, thy spells did bind
To fear himself, and love all humankind.''

Idle yearning of a lawless sentimentalism, the poetic prayer may seem to those who consider religion a hard, rough, and abrasive legality; but in Shelley's soul this sentimentalism had more than the force and did the full work of law. Beauty swayed every impulse of his being. Though passing storms sometimes vexed its surface, its deep, constant tides always obeyed Beauty's mild and lunar persuasion. He loved physi-

cal pleasure, not with a bestial appetite and relish, but because and only to the extent in which it was beautiful to his
senses. He loved Truth because it was beautiful to his reason ; benevolence, because it was beautiful to his sympathies ;
right, duty, goodness, because they were beautiful to his conscience.

And if to govern passion by temperance; to shun falsehood
with abhorrence; to follow conviction without hesitancy or
regretful looking back even when it leads away from friends,
fortune, title and good report, and offers no compensation but
a cross of calumny; to esteem the happiness of others above
one's own; to go through temptation not unscathed of evil
but untainted with constitutional vice, keeping the soul faithful as a maiden-knight betrothed to its own San Gréal; if
this be religion—then was Shelley's a thoroughly and bravely
religious character—all the more so because he fulfilled the
law from love alone and without the stimulating expectation
of immortal wages.

His views of marriage were, doubtless, immoral in their
tendencies, but they cannot on that account be construed as
a sign of immorality in his character. To know the truth
does not demonstrate virtue, nor to be ignorant of it, vice.
Knowledge of truth is often the result of educational good
luck or of rare endowments of intellect, without implying the
exercise of courage, resolution, self-denial or any distinctively
moral trait; whereas, the adoption of error may end a life-long
endeavor to avoid it—an·endeavor which in noble sincerity
has forsaken beliefs once dear, wrestled with doubts, borne
reproach, suffered almost daily martyrdom. It is the love of
truth, not the knowledge of it, which is moral; and by this
test Shelley's character should be judged. Was he honest
in the formation of his opinions and diligent in his search of
the evidences which should determine them? If so, not to

confess them in his conduct, however odious that conduct would appear to the public, may have been prudence or cowardice, but certainly was not morality.

Shelley's mistake consisted in transferring the ideal life of a perfect society to the conditions of one malformed and mischievous. Since in an Elysium of humanity no laws or rites would be necessary to control personal action, that action being prompted by the impulse of a pure heart wishing the welfare of all, and all being harmonized by the prevalence of the same wise and supreme sentiment of equity— Shelley imagined that he ought to set an example of independence of laws and rites in his own behavior. He failed to consider that his ethical relations were not with the end of the world but with the England of his own day and, that in the absence of the conditions which alone could warrant perfect spontaneity of life, such life was not only unobligatory, but sure to be pernicious.

When Shelley eloped with Harriet Westbrook, they were both little more than children and neither believed in marriage as an indissoluble bond unless the hearts it united grew together as one. In their case it proved a tie of antagonisms, and they parted with mutual consent. For Helen's subsequent and tragic fall Shelley cannot be held accountable. Enough that it was the fall of the star Wormwood into the sweet waters of his new love, turning them to bitterness. In Mary Godwin he met the only woman, perhaps, of his time who could sympathize with his morbid nature and share its most visionary moods. Herself the offspring of celebrated parents who had abjured all other bonds of matrimony than unconstrained agreement, and educated in their way of thinking, she consented to partake his obloquy and pain. It was a happy union—that is to say, as happy as any could be which began partly in distress of heart and continued under the scorn of society. As far as evidence reveals, Shelley was true to its affiance. The erotic poems which seem to indicate other loves are pure idealizations—one of them an allegory of his own soul and its desires, the other a souvenir dedicated to a lady who received none of his writings except through the hand of her husband, his best friend in life and his comrade in death. In accordance with the refinement of their theme, which was not so much the persons they addressed as certain ideal qualities represented by those persons, neither of the poems contains a hint of flesh-and-blood sensuality. Indeed, sensuality is the last charge that with any show of plausibility can be brought against this soul which, whatever its eccentricities of belief or action, stood so high above mean aims and gross passions, that even Byron in his mad career of license avouched with a tinge of enthusiasm in his words—

"Shelley was the most gentle, the most amiable, the least worldly-minded person I ever met; full of delicacy; disinterested beyond all other men, and possessing a degree of genius joined to a simplicity as rare as it is admirable. He had formed to himself a beau-ideal of all that is fine, high-minded, and noble, and he acted up to this ideal even to the very letter."

Such was the poet in his twenty-seventh year when about to undertake his coronal work. He had seen, read, and studied much. He had consulted the great oracles of all ages—Homer, Plato, the Greek dramatists, Moschus, Virgil, Dante, Tasso, Calderon, Goethe, and by translating their speech into his own, had guaged his ability of expressing fairest and sublimest thought. He had charmed his heedless countrymen with lyrics which convinced them that the mind they regarded a dusky and tangled brake of delusions was nevertheless the home of a nightingale. He had, moreover, essayed an epic which, thickly sown with splendors of description, wanted only symmetery of plan to render them a world-known constellation. And if

"Most wretched men
Are cradled into poetry by wrong

And learn in suffering what they teach in song,"

he had received from that severe poetic discipline a competent training. And now he "will do something which a serious and earnest estimate of his powers has suggested and which shall be in every respect accommodated to their utmost limits."

So at Rome, amid the flowery glades that flourish on the ruined baths of Caracalla, under a roof of bright blue sky, and with every sense and faculty intoxicated by the atmosphere of Spring, he begins Prometheus Unbound. There, day after day, may be seen his tall spare form sitting on the mossy lawn which overspreads the mosaic pavement of the upper walls and arches, the brown hair too early streaked with gray, falling in thick curls on a pensive forehead, the girlish face flushed as if 'radiant apparitions' were wooing his genius, and the hand quick with its record as if eager to fix their fading discourse in periods that can never grow dim.

It is a well-chosen trysting-place for Shelley and Poetry. Desolation is there to tell of the havocs of the Past, and Nature's latest bloom to remind how ever out of death springs richer life, and over all a glorious climate to forecast the Promethean Age of Mankind.

To say no more than that the poem is extraordinary which absorbs these influences and grows by them into a consummate symbol of Divine humanity, were to detract from its least merit. To say that in certain respects it is the most wonderful of poems, is to incur the suspicion of extravagance, usually excited by superlatives. But where else will you find such cosmic might of imagination condensing diffusest nebulæ of mind into a world of dream with landscapes clear as ever delighted eye of flesh yet so phantasmal, it seems, the jar of a sunbeam would dissolve them—

"Dim twilight lawns and stream-illumined caves

And wind-enchanted shapes of wandering mist
And far on high the keen sky-cleaving mountains—"

all peopled with 'terrible, strange, sublime, and beauteous' forms, bodied from no common dust of invention, but born of the subtilest aura of fantasy and with the breath of Orphic song in their lips?

Where else will you find such flights of speculation exploring height above height the remotest firmaments of mystery without a tiresome strain or dull droop of wing, up to the empyrean that overlooks the whole round of time complete at last in man delivered from the torture of evil and emparadised in the felicities of his own free spirit—

> " Equal, unclassed, tribeless and nationless,
> Exempt from awe, worship, degree, the King
> Over himself; just, gentle, wise ; but man,
> Passionless? no :—yet free from guilt and pain—
> Which were, for his will made or suffered them ;
> Nor yet exempt, though ruling them like slaves,
> From chance and death and mutability,—
> The clogs of that which else might oversoar
> The loftiest star of unascended heaven
> Pinnacled dim in the intense inane."

Fault has been found with the poem because of its lack of human incidents and passions, but unreasonably, for these would be incongruous to its design. It has nothing to do with the individual or his life. It is a drama of the race. Its scenery and plot pertain to a generic mind, which has the peculiarities of no family, tribe, or nation, but spreads through all humanity and endures through all epochs. By the ignorance of this mind Evil was created and then deified. The propensions of this mind Evil has turned to tormenting furies of

> " Pain and fear
> And disappointment and mistrust and hate
> And clinging crime."

The very best aspirations of this mind—its love and hope and worship—Evil has thwarted of their true aim and duped into his own unrecognized service of fanaticism and woe—

> " The good want power but to weep barren tears;
> The powerful goodness want—worse need for them ;
> The wise want love ; and those who love want wisdom ;
> And all best things are thus confused to ill."

But, on the other side, in the hope and love of this mind lives a fortitude which Evil cannot utterly crush, and in its knowledge grows a strength which all the sufferings sent by Evil to subdue it only invigorate and weapon for the blow that at last hurls the Arch-Usurper from his throne.

Thus, from beginning to end, the drama seeks to enact itself within a purely subjective realm which admits nothing from the outside. The intrusion of an earthly character would mar its speculative integrity. The Divina Commedia may have the five fraudulent counselors of Florence swathing themselves from recognition with the flames of its Malebolge, and a Beatrice illuminating its Paradise with her smile—for Dante's are a hell and heaven of individual retribution and reward. Faust may have its pedantic Wagner and tipsy Frostch, and heart-broken Marguerite singing crazy snatches of ballads in her dungeon—for Goethe's is an earth of individual longing, endeavor, disappointment and self conquest. But Shelley's world must, at all risks of obscurity, unreality, absence of adventure, exclude the individual and outward from its transcendental scenes. Its inhabitants must be spectral, often formless, sometimes only voices; its hero a ' writhing shadow 'mid whirlwind-peopled mountains, its Demogorgon—impersonating Necessity—a tremendous gloom.'

Evidently a poem so unique in conception cannot be properly judged by standards adopted from masterpieces of an entirely different kind. Are its sentiments strange and mystical? They are anticipations of a sublimer humanity than now exists, and move on a level with its altitude. Are the images difficult to interpret?—they are attempts to cast hueless and formless ideas into colors and shapes of sense. Are the speculations perplexed with excessive allegory?—in a drama where the actors are all abstractions and many of the scenes are pictured phases of a cosmogony, it is scarcely possible to confine allegorical action within an average of popular ability to understand it. No doubt there are passages that need explanation and baffle any effort to discover their esoteric import, but such have generally a double meaning—a form of beauty as well as a secret of philosophy, and should the latter be missed, the former will delight. Take, for illustration, the whole of the second Act. It represents the flight of Asia and Panthea to the throne of Demogorgon and thence to a vision of man's future Eden. They pass through landscapes of matchless beauty, and hear music so sweet that the joy of listening is almost pain. The landscapes are shown with a finish of detail and vividness of coloring that make the poet's words seem stereoscopic of realities, and the music breathes out of the lines that describe it as out of the opening stops of a flute. But all the while this flight sybolizes an argument for the progress and perfectibility of mankind. The argument is Necessity—Nature's primal law—the inevitable relation of antecedent and consequent which renders every thought, word and deed as persistent and per-petual in their influence as the forces that formed and are yet forming the earth; and as these forces have evolved order out of chaos, life out of death, and spirit out of clay, so the wise thought, the true word, and the good deed, by the im-perishable power within them, shall countervail the Evil of temporary ignorance and falsehood, and produce the perfect race.

It is while in search of this prophetic law that Asia and Panthea pass through a forest full of eddying sounds; the delicate music represents the spiral play of the forces of growth in the trees—forces which have various modes of manifestation, but are one and the same in air, and water, and earth, and therefore it may be said of them in their molecular fay-like movements, that

> " The bubbles, which the enchantment of the sun
> Sucks from the pale faint water-flowers that pave
> The oozy bottom of clear lakes and pools,
> Are the pavillons where such dwell and float
> Under the green and golden atmosphere
> Which noontide kindles through the woven leaves,
> And when these burst, and the thin fiery air
> The which they breathed within those lucent domes,
> Ascends to flow like meteors through the night
> They ride on them, and rein their headlong speed,
> And bow their burning crests, and glide in fire
> Under the waters of the earth again."

But the search goes deeper than the mysteries of external Nature—

> Down, Down !
> Through the shade of Sleep,
> Through the cloudy strife
> Of Death and of Life;
> Through the veil and the bar
> Of things which seem and are
> Even to the steps of the remotest throne,
> Down, Down."

The throne types the universal reign of law. This consulted, the Immortal Hours are seen driving by, and last of their *cortege* appears one whose chariot is

> "An ivory shell inlaid with crimson fire,
> Which comes and goes within its sculptured rim
> Of delicate strange tracery."

He is the Hour with 'dove-like eyes of hope'—the foreseen

hour of man's rescue from immemorial bondage—and conducts the flight of argument on to its grand conclusion—

"We have passed Age's icy caves,
And Manhood's dark and tossing waves,
And Youth's smooth ocean, smiling to betray ;
Beyond the glassy gulfs we flee
Of shadow-peopled Infancy,
Through Death and Birth, to a diviner day."

To be duly esteemed Prometheus Unbound must not only
be read but studied—studied with a modest disposition to
think that what appears its author's mysticism may be the
student's mistiness of apprehension—studied with an effort to
learn the ideas which its characters personify and thereby
to interpret their discourse—studied with the recollection
that it is throughout an allegory and that its most realistic
passages preserve the allegorical continuity of its plan. Thus
studied in addition to the music and painting and colossal
sculpture of impersonation which the most careless reading
acknowledges to be wonderful—it will disclose a breadth and
depth and height of philosophy that make it the Epic of
Modern Thought.

Poetry of sense may be a pastime—smooth sleigh-driving
to a jangle of bells—but Poetry has other offices than amuse-
ment. Her noblest work is to elevate, to make the goal of
the past the starting point of the future, to remove the ideals
of the race further and further onward and aloft. She is the
seer of possibilities and the forerunner of progress. All
that is known of beauty, wisdom, power, and goodness lie
beneath her feet, which stand upon the loftiest summit of
reason, whence she gazes down only for likenesses that may
limn to those who dwell below, the heavenly vision she alone
can see.

Hence that poem is greatest which, like a mountain, having
all climes of sentiment on its slopes, rises to peaks of ideal-

ization unattainable without the Alp-climber's circumspect eye and tense exertion. And such a poem, though it springs with the steepness of a crag into the region of clouds, is Prometheus Unbound.

Fifty years have gone by since Shelley sank into the Mediterranean; and his genius, contemned while pent within his youthful form, is now seen dilating the stature of our century. His odes are the marching-hymns of science. His wild dreams of reform are fast sobering into fulfillment. Many of the laws that angered him against the government of his native land, have been repealed, and others lie as impotent as death upon its statute-books. The liberty which he hailed from afar has drawn near; the lightnings of her eyes have become familiar, and nation after nation, once blinded by their lustre, is learning to bear their look and soon shall rejoice in it as an angel's look of blessing.

R. A. HOLLAND.

THE ILIAD

BOOK I.

Jove to persistent Thetis nods,
Great Juno chides. Feast of the Gods.

Thus she spake. But to her, Jove, Cloud Compeller, replied not.
Nay, he long sat silent. But Thêtis, as first she his knees clasped,
So, she, clinging, held ; and again she further besought him :
" Faithfully, even Infallibly, pledge me !—Yea, nod me a promise !
Else refuse—for no god is near—and assuredly show me
How much more than all am I, though a goddess, dishonored."
Cloud-Compelling Jove then answered her, heavily sighing :
"Woeful the task—alas !—for thou dost command me to madden
Juno, when she shall anger me with her contemptuous speeches ;
520 And she, 'mong the immortal Divinities ever at me thus
Raileth, and chargeth that I give aid to the Trojans in battle.
Nay, now, thou withdraw thee at once, nor suffer to see thee
Juno ; and I will attend to this, and secure its fulfillment.
Come !—if thou doubt, with the nod will I promise, that thou mayst
      believe me !
Sithence that this from me is with the Immortals the highest
Evidence : sithence that neither retracted, neither deceptive,
Neither shall be unexecute, what with the nod I may promise."
Yea !—and with his cerulean brows the Saturnian nodded !
Then flowed undulant down the ambrosial locks of the Ruler—
530 Sovereign from the eterne ! And mighty Olympus was shaken !
They twain, counseling thus, disparted. She, in an instant,
Into the depths of the salt sea leaped from shining Olympus.
But to his dome went Jove. And at once rose all the Divine Ones
From their thrones, at the sight of the Father ; nor any one ventured
His approach to await, but all arose at his entrance.
Thus, then, sat he down on his throne. Yet he not from Juno
Hidden had been, for she witnessed when with him united in counsel
Thetis the Silver Foot, child of the Ancient One of the Salt Sea.
Then, with words heart-piercing, to Jove the Saturnian spake she :
540   " Which of the gods has been joining in counsel with you, you
      Deceiver ?